Sophie and the Shofar

· A NEW YEAR'S STORY ·

Fran Manushkin

illustrated by

Rosalind Charney Kaye

UAHC Press   ·   New York

For Sophie Maya Mann —FM

To Nick on his eighteenth birthday,
with all my love —RCK

Library of Congress Cataloging-in-Publication Data

Manushkin, Fran.
Sophie and the shofar / Fran Manushkin ;
illustrated by Rosalind Charney Kaye.
p. cm.
Summary: After describing some of the traditions of
Rosh Hashanah, the Jewish New Year, to her cousin from Russia,
Sophie learns about trust and forgiveness.
ISBN 0-8074-0761-8 (cloth : alk. paper)
[1. Rosh ha-Shanah—Fiction. 2. Fasts and feasts—Judaism—Fiction.
3. Jews—United States—Fiction. 4. New Year—Fiction. 5. Cousins—
Fiction.] I. Kaye, Rosalind Charney, ill. II. Title.

PZ7.M3195 So 2001   00-066680
[E]—dc21

Text copyright © 2001 by Fran Manushkin
Illustrations © 2001 by Rosalind Charney Kaye
Manufactured in the United States of America
10 9 8 7 6 5 4 3 2 1

*T*his is how it happens every year: When the leaves on our maple tree turn from green to red, and the sheets on my bed change from plain to flannel, I know it's almost time for Rosh HaShanah, the Jewish New Year, when we celebrate the birthday of the world.

Well, *this* year, something horrible happened, and I'm going to tell you all about it.

A month ago, Papa said to me, "Guess what, Sophie? Your cousin Sasha is moving in next door." Sasha has fuzzy red hair and he's from Russia, and he's noisy in two languages.

The first week after Sasha moved next door, we went roller-blading. Usually, I don't go too fast, but Sasha grabbed my hand, and we whooshed along the sidewalk like tornadoes.

"In Russia, the ground is not so smooth!" Sasha shouted. *"Ya-hoo!"*

"Ya-hoo!" I yelled too. It was fun being noisy with Sasha.

The next day, I showed Sasha how to stuff his shirt with leaves and become a monster. We took turns scaring each other, sneaking up and yelling, "Boo!"

A few days later, Papa told me, "Sophie, back in Russia, Sasha's family didn't know how to celebrate the New Year. Why don't you show him what we do?"

"Sure," I said. I got out my watercolors and showed Sasha how we make New Year cards. I drew a Star of David, and then Sasha drew one, only much bigger.

Then I drew a big one too.

"Big is better!" Sasha said, and I agreed. I had never made such a big card before. But just as I was going to show Sasha how we sprinkle the Star of David with glitter, we heard a loud noise coming from the den.

"What's that?" Sasha asked.

"Oh," I answered, "that's Papa practicing the shofar."

"What is a shofar?" Sasha asked.

"Come, I'll show you." I said, and I took him into the den.

Papa explained to Sasha, "A shofar is a ram's horn. Each year we blow it in synagogue, to begin the New Year."

Sasha grinned and his eyes lit up. "You can make *noise*— in synagogue?"

"Yes!" Papa smiled back. "The louder the shofar, the better!" Papa made such a racket, my dog, Farfel, hid under a chair, covering his ears with his paws.

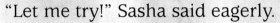

"Let me try!" Sasha said eagerly.

Papa shook his head. "This ram's horn is a hundred years old. My papa played it, and before him, my grandfather. No one touches this horn but *me*."

Sasha got grumpy then. I tried to cheer him up. "Let's go finish our cards," I said. But he made a face, and then he left—just like that.

I ended up finishing the cards all alone.

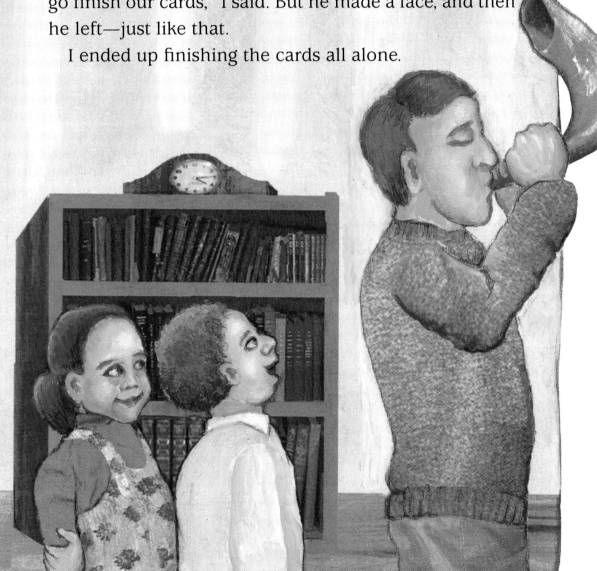

The next day, Sasha came over in the middle of bread baking.

"You can help me," I told him. "Your big fists are perfect for pounding the dough. On Rosh HaShanah, we eat round challah bread dipped in honey, to make sure we have a sweet year."

"Sweet? I love sweets!" Sasha said in his happy, noisy voice, and he grabbed some dough and began to pound it. *"Poomph!"* He panted, grunting like a bear.

"Poomph!" I grunted, and giggled. Everything was so much fun with Sasha.

Farfel didn't like the racket we were making. He ran outside to bury a bone.

But right in the middle of pounding, Sasha suddenly stopped. Why? Because Papa was practicing the shofar again. Sasha put down the dough and ran into the den. "Let *me* play!" Sasha begged.

"No," said Papa, refusing. "I told you before. *Nobody* plays the shofar but me."

Sasha's face fell. He wanted to play it so much.

"Come on, let's finish the bread," I said. But Sasha couldn't stop thinking about that shofar, and when he pounded the dough, he dropped it—*PLOP!*—on the floor.

"Look what you did!" I yelled.

Sasha shouted back, "Bread is stupid!" Then he ran out the door, leaving *me* to clean up the mess. Boy, I was getting really mad at him!

The next day, after school, when I saw Sasha walking home, I made a face at him and ran away. That showed him.

The day after that, when I came home from school, there was Sasha, standing in the kitchen. His face turned red when he saw me, and he hid his hands behind his back. Then he ran out the door!

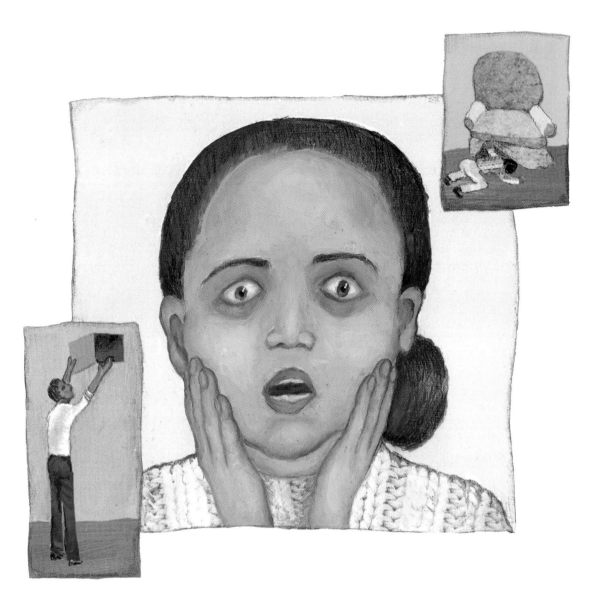

Right after this, Papa came home to practice the shofar. He went into the den, but a minute later, he came out again. "Where's my shofar?" he asked. "I can't find it."

We searched the den and then the whole house, but we couldn't find the shofar anywhere.

Then I remembered Sasha's red face—and his hands hidden behind his back. "Sasha took the shofar!" I told Papa.

"He would *never* do that," Papa said.

But I ran next door to Sasha's house, and yelled at him, "You took our shofar! Give it back right now!"

"I didn't take it!" Sasha insisted. "I didn't!"

"You're a liar! I hate you!" I yelled. "Why don't you go back to Russia!" I'll never forget the look on Sasha's face. He looked like he was about to cry.

The next night was the beginning of Rosh HaShanah. As we ate our dinner, Papa sighed, "What are we going to do? We can't have the holiday without the shofar."

The next morning, we began the short walk to synagogue. Farfel tried to follow us, but I said, "Go home!"

As soon as we reached the synagogue, all the kissing began. "*Shanah Tovah*! Happy New Year!" beamed Grandpa.

I could see Sasha coming with his mother and father. "He'd better stay far away from me," I told Mama.

Papa rushed over to tell Rabbi Cowan the bad news about the shofar, but before he could open his mouth, Rabbi Cowan told him, "Remember to clasp the horn tightly when you blow it. You don't want to drop it!"

"I have to tell you—" Papa began, but Cantor Engel interrupted to tell Papa, "Be sure to take a deep breath when you blow the shofar. If you don't, only a wheeze will come out."

Then everyone hurried inside, so what could we do? We went inside too.

Right away, I snuggled deep inside Papa's silky white prayer shawl. When I poked my head out a minute later, I saw Sasha—right at the end of our row!

His fuzzy hair was brushed flat, and he wore a nice suit. When he saw me, I pinched my lips together tight and looked away.

Rabbi Cowan started speaking. She said, "As this year
ends, we should all think about our actions, and if we have
harmed anybody, we must ask their forgiveness."

"I hope that horrible Sasha's listening," I told myself. I
looked around and saw Sasha looking at me. I stuck out my
tongue.

It's hard to pray after sticking out your tongue, but I tried.
I prayed hard that someone would find Papa's shofar.

Suddenly there was a noisy rustle and giggles from the back of the synagogue. I whirled around in my seat, and what did I see? Farfel running toward me—with the shofar in his mouth!

"Farfel, you found the shofar!"

"Look," Papa said, pointing at the dirt on the ram's horn. "Farfel hated the racket I made with the shofar, so he buried it like a bone."

I giggled. "And now he's dug it up again—just in time for the holiday!"

As Papa rushed away to wash off the shofar, I sat back down again. That's when I felt an awful ache in my stomach, and my face grew hot, flushing red. Sasha! I had been so mean to him! All the terrible words I'd said came rushing back to me.

The colors in the stained-glass window grew blurry, because tears were filling my eyes. I left my seat, and went over to Sasha, and told him, "I'm so sorry!"

Sasha's face broke into the happiest smile, and he said, "I'm sorry too." Then he handed me an envelope. "*This* is what I was hiding behind my back when you saw me in your kitchen." Inside the envelope was a beautiful card that said, "I'm sorry, Sophie!"

"Thank you," I beamed at him. "Sasha, promise me, you won't go back to Russia."

"I promise!" He grinned.

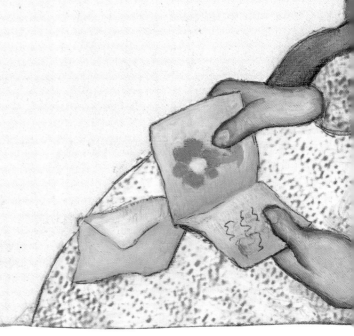

Soon, everyone in synagogue grew very quiet. Papa raised the shofar to his lips—and out came a mighty blast! It was so loud, it made the chandelier shake.

Papa blew short blasts, and he blew long blasts. Then it was time for the last one. It had to be the longest and loudest—so that our year would start off nice and *strong*.

Papa took a deep breath, and so did everyone else. Papa's long note went on and *on* . . .

Only when the last echo faded did we breathe again. Later, we all hugged and said, "*Shanah Tovah*! Happy New Year!" You can't say it too many times.

After the service, Papa came over to Sasha and said, "I've been thinking, and I realize I was *wrong* not to let you play the shofar. So I'm going to teach you how."

"Me too?" I asked.

"Sure," Papa agreed.

"Poor Farfel," Sasha grinned. "He's going to hate it!"

I laughed, and then I whispered in Mama's ear, "Can Sasha's family have Rosh HaShanah supper with us?"

"Of course," Mama nodded. "I already invited them."

    As we walked home from synagogue, Papa said, "Sasha, Sophie, did you know that on the High Holy Days, the gates of heaven are open? If you watch the sky closely, you might see an angel."

    "An angel?" Sasha beamed. "*This* I have to see."

    "Me too!" I shouted. So all the way home, we kept our eyes on the sky. Did we see any angels? *I'll* never tell. You'll have to look for yourself!